ENCOUNTER WITH A WISE MAN

A Christmas Tale of Wisdom

Encounter with a Wise Man

A Christmas Tale of Wisdom

by

Paul T Kidd

Cheshire Henbury

First published in 2012 by Cheshire Henbury as part of a trilogy of short stories. Published in this edition as an individual short story in 2013. ISBN 978-1-901864-14-4

British Library Cataloguing in Publication Data.
A catalogue record for this book is available from the British Library.

Cheshire Henbury
E-mail: books@cheshirehenbury.com

Web site: www.cheshirehenbury.com/encounterwithawiseman

Dedicated to those who suffer as a consequence of ideology and dogma, in whatever form this comes: political, economic, religious or scientific. Surely it is time to stop this madness.

PREFACE

Encounter with a Wise Man is a tale based on a meeting between two mythical characters: Balthazar (one of the three wise men of the nativity story) and Father Christmas. This is the seasonal aspect of the book, and in the reading of it may the contents add to your festive feelings. But the book also has a more serious purpose related to that which we call wisdom.

What is wisdom? This is wisdom: take the time to find out for yourself, for I cannot tell you. Let me explain a small amount to help you understand this statement. A dictionary definition of wisdom will typically describe it as an ability to make good decisions based on both knowledge and experience. This, it could be said, is also typical in another sense, it being the product of the western mind, with its focus on rational logical thought, which has little to offer when it comes to understanding wisdom.

So, rather than seeking out the definition that resolves, once and for all, the meaning of wisdom, let that place in your mind where your humanity resides take charge, and think about relationships, emotions, feelings, empathy and the like. If you do this, then you are moving towards an understanding of wisdom, for wisdom is most definitely not about allowing the dominance of the rational. And here are some words and phrases to help you in your quest: deeper understandings, insights, the bigger picture, perceptions, intuition, humility, compassion, accepting ambiguity, contemplation and reflection, the limits of knowledge, seeing things from many perspectives, tolerance, more than one way, more than one answer, and so forth.

So I repeat my message: I will not tell you what wisdom is, for I cannot tell you what wisdom is. And if you are uncomfortable with this message, read this book and start to reflect upon the reasons why you need to change.

Now I return to the matter of this book, and what motivated the writing of the tale here recounted for you. And what was this motivation? The answer is simple: a self-evident observation that wisdom is now often absent from contemporary civilisation, and increasingly so! In other words, as the condition of the planet, our societies, and the economic system deteriorates, we are becoming even less inclined to be wise, preferring instead to push ahead and continue doing those things that are responsible for the decline in the first place.

You doubt perhaps that this is the case? You are free to do so, for optimism is part of human nature, and it is good and positive to be optimistic. Optimism, however, as Voltaire put it, is a mania for insisting that all is well when all is by no means well. This, I think, well summarises the lunatic asylum in which we are now living; you will know this mad-house better by the label, *the modern world.*

This book is an invitation to reflect upon the insight that most of what is wrong with the world in which we live is a result of the actions of the children of ideology; specifically, those who adhere to the dogmas associated with religion, the free-market economy, and science (and its close relatives engineering and technology). These children, believing that they are engaged in some heroic struggle to construct the best of all possible worlds, but without any regard for that which makes us human, may be building the walls of a prison in which humanity will find itself incarcerated for eternity. This may turn out to be the true hell on earth; a place where many of those end-of-world apocalyptic prophecies, which from time to time are mentioned in the popular press, may seem like attractive options.

But do not misunderstand me, for I am not against religion, free-market economics, and science; it is just that they are not fit for purpose, and need to evolve. Key to this evolution is the development of spirituality and wisdom in those who would practise in these domains, and this applies to those who are religious as much as to anyone else.

So what of the ultimate point of my story? This is quite simple: to help people to understand that there is a choice – the world does not have to be the way the children of ideology would have it be. The free-thinking peoples of the world should not let this happen, and what better time of the year is there than Christmas, a time for salvation and redemption, to reflect upon such matters? People should not let those with ideological agendas determine our future and that of our planet.

It is time to change religion, free-market economics and science, and to begin to construct a sustainable civilisation – time for humanity to begin to walk a different path. How to do this, however, is another matter; one that is dealt with in other writings.

Paul T Kidd
June 2013

"Optimism is a mania for insisting that all is well when all is by no means well"
Voltaire (*Candide*)

"Men's courses will foreshadow certain ends, to which, if persevered in they must lead ..., but if the courses be departed from the ends will change"
Charles Dickens (*A Christmas Carol*)

"Two roads diverged in a wood and I - I took the one less travelled by, and that has made all the difference"
Robert Frost ("The Road Not Taken")

Encounter with a Wise Man

You have all heard, I feel sure, of the three wise men who journeyed from the east to the small town of Bethlehem. This is an enduring aspect to the nativity story – three wise, and, presumably, wealthy individuals, undertaking a long and arduous journey, and mostly likely a dangerous one too. And what of the purpose of this extended and challenging voyage across deserts and mountains? This, as we all know, was to pay homage to a baby born of humble parents, in the poorest of settings; for these wise men knew, or at least strongly suspected, that this child was more than just one more human born into a world of suffering and strife, intermingled with moments of joy, happiness, and love, as is the way of life.

I will tell you here that what I am about to reveal to you concerns an encounter with one of these wise men – my tale is based on an unexpected and very unusual meeting. In these so-called modern times, where life is bound up with the apparent sophistication that comes from having many wonderful artefacts in our lives (that is to say of course, compared with circumstances 2,000 years ago when the events that I am about to reveal took place), it is far harder to believe in that which has no physical form, or that which involves mysteries that cannot be fathomed through a scientific approach. In the modern world, the utility of human endeavours has to be counted in terms of making life materially better, or its contribution to supposedly laying bare the mysteries of the universe, or running our lives faster and more efficiently as though we are all little businesses, where time is money, but where there is no time for that which really matters.

It is, indeed, a long way from the deserts of the past to the modern cities of the present. Perhaps it is a measure of how far humankind has fallen that it was so easy for those who dwelt in the deserts of the world to believe and to be wise! But what exactly am I referring to? This question is more profound than it may seem, for I am not talking just about belief in God. Let me elucidate before embarking on my most intriguing story.

I will keep this explanation short. You will, no doubt, have encountered some person on your journey through life who talks and thinks only in very limited terms and frames of reference. There are those who expound the virtues of the free-market enterprise, believing in unrestricted and unregulated markets, and the freedom to make money in just about any way they can, despite the consequences. There are those who expound narrow religious dogma, believing that they, and only they and those who share their beliefs, are the sole source of the truth, being intolerant of those with different philosophies and beliefs. And there are those who operate in the realms of science, or engineering, or technology, who claim to think in terms of facts, or that which can be proven, and who would represent the world, and those who dwell in it, as nothing more that mechanistic artefacts, capable of being, ultimately, fully understood and explained (and also, perhaps, controlled, or even replaced).

Most of these people, regardless of their perspectives – be they economic, religious, or scientific – share one trait in common: they are ideological, although none of them would recognise this, they being *too clever by half* to fall into such a trap. And, being caught up in a way of thinking and viewing the world that they do not even recognise as ideological, they account for persons with different and opposing perspectives as suffering from some deficit, from a lack of *right-mindedness*. For all their apparent sophistication, and in some cases intelligence and education, many ideologically inclined people, through their thoughts and actions, would reduce the lives of us all to a living hell. These ideologues can be very dangerous people, yet you might not immediately think so, and what can be said about many such characters is that they are not *wise*, which brings me back to my tale of the wise man and what he told me, which I here recount for you.

~

"It was our prediction of the conjunction of Saturn and Jupiter that first alerted us to the events that were eventually to unfold in Bethlehem," the wise man stated, as though such prophecies were an everyday occurrence in his world.

"Let me introduce myself. I am Balthazar, and the *we* of which I speak are my fellow scholars, Melchior and Caspar.

"Perhaps you think that I am about to recall the long journey that we undertook, all those thousands of years ago, and that I am about to describe our encounter with that miraculous child; but do not worry for I have no intention of boring you with a tale which I am sure you know all too well.

"I see by the look on your face that your curiosity is aroused. How can this be? Have you encountered a lunatic? Balthazar is long dead. No-one is immortal.

"I would myself have agreed with you, long ago, when, in that far distant age, I first set off for Bethlehem. Let me explain, for this is at the heart of my story.

"Let us move forward, to the stage where we were about to depart from Bethlehem. Up to this point, you know my tale. It is what follows next that nobody is aware of, for it is a well-kept secret. Here I will clarify for you that Melchior and Caspar are both dead, for what occurred to me did not happen to them. So life took its course and they, like all men, passed out of the physical world, into the next, but how and when that took place I do not know, as you will soon understand.

"There we were, just leaving, and also aware that we could not go back the same way we had come, for there was immense evil afoot in the form of that corrupt and dangerous man called Herod. Of this you are fully aware from the telling of our story so many, many, times.

"So we discussed the matter and decided upon our course of action. Thinking that we might be followed by Herod's agents, or waylaid by them in some remote and isolated place, we decided that it would be safer for the baby whom we were leaving behind, if each of us to travelled separately, and to make our way back home by different routes. This would make following us more difficult, as Herod would not have considered this in his diabolical plans. But, of course, we knew that travelling alone would be more dangerous for us, but this was a risk we were willing to take, such was the importance of the child we had just visited.

"As we had come by a road from the east, and this was most probably where Herod's men would hide and wait for us, we decided that Melchior would travel west, Caspar would go south, and I would journey north. Thus it was that we set off, going our separate ways, and I was never to see Melchior and Caspar again.

"My journey was, at first, uneventful. My plan was to keep moving northwards, and then, after a few days, to turn in an easterly direction for a while, and then head southeast until I arrived back in my own lands. But my plans were thwarted, for, as I was soon to discover, my destiny lay elsewhere.

"Three days out from Bethlehem, I was passing through a very remote and uninhabited area. The landscape here was very undulating and it was not always possible to see what lay ahead, or behind for that matter. But the features of my surroundings provided me with the ability to travel without being observed.

"During the daylight hours I rested, while under cover of darkness I made good progress northward. In the far north I could see a mountain range with snow-covered peaks, and it was out of these mountains that it came.

"At first I thought it was a shooting star, for it was no more than a very small point of light, leaving a tiny sparkling trail in its wake. But I soon realised that I was wrong, since this object was growing larger and heading directly towards me!

"In a matter of a few moments it was there in front of me, hovering above the ground, and what a splendid sight it was. I will not recount to you the full details, lest I become tedious by providing information that I know you are familiar with. I was not aware at that moment in time exactly by what name this artefact is known, but it was a sleigh, pulled by creatures which I now know are called reindeer, and sitting inside this magical mode of transport was a man dressed in red.

"You of course know who this was, but I did not. However, I had seen this person before.

"Here I will briefly explain. When we visited that stable in Bethlehem, we were not the only visitors, as there were, as you are aware, also some shepherds present. But what you do not know is that there were also other folk who came and went that night, and none more mysterious than a man who just seemed to step out of thin air, dressed in a bright-green, hooded cloak and wearing furs. Self-evidently he was from a land where the climate was much colder than that of the region in which most of us dwelt.

"I will also tell you that when he departed, his clothes had changed colour, and he was dressed in red. This, of course, is part of the legend of how Father Christmas came to be, but I will not recount here the details, although some of that story has a bearing on my own tale.

"Back now to the account of events that took place on that night, when, quite unexpectedly, and by magical means, Father Christmas appeared to me. Imagine the scene. I am standing with my camel, looking in awe at this wondrous flying machine, within which sits this jovial man dressed in red. He beckons to me to approach the sleigh, and this I do for I have no fear, as within me there is a feeling of joy and happiness. He then tells me to set free my camel and to come with him. This again I do without question. I will tell you also that I had no concerns about my camel, for these are, at heart, wild creatures of the desert lands. Freed from carrying my possessions and with the saddle removed, it would naturally find its way to places where other camels dwelt, and this is exactly what happened.

"In a moment, we were flying high through the sky, and this I should tell you was an exciting experience, for never before had men in my age flown, and the view of the world below, even though it was dark, was thrilling. Then we were in the mountains that I have already mentioned, and we came to a halt, settling down in a small valley between two jagged peaks. And, although it was cold so high up in these mountains, and snow lay all about, we were not at all chilled by this winter weather, for inside the sleigh it was very warm indeed, such was the magic of this curious mode of transport.

"Immediately, Father Christmas began to speak, explaining what was happening and why, and what my future entailed. He spoke of my destiny. Being an astrologer, I knew of such matters and I was well attuned to the notion of fate, thus I listened carefully and with interest, knowing that he spoke not for himself, but for someone far greater.

"I will distil for you the essence of what was told to me that night, for to tell you all, word for word, would take far too long, and I know that you are most likely very busy, being a person of the modern world.

"It all rested on one aspect of my life, which was that I, being a scholar with knowledge of astrology and alchemy, was a learned person.

"I know what you are thinking – astrology and alchemy are nonsense. Of course, you have been conditioned by scientific thinking, so I can understand such a sentiment; there is no place in such a sophisticated society as yours for suppositious beliefs, except perhaps among hippies and other fringe groups lacking in *right-minded thinking*. Astrology and alchemy, you believe, belong in the past, when people knew no better. Today, people are aware of how to discover facts, because they adhere to the scientific method. But can you really discern truth, or are you locked into a philosophy which blinds you to aspects of reality that cannot be understood through science alone? Would the great Isaac

Newton, that iconic figure of the Scientific Revolution, even recognise what you today have come to think of as science?

"I will not seek to defend astrology and alchemy. All I will say is that these were part of the age into which I was born, and these arts fulfilled a need. But, in those far distant times, astrology and alchemy were not what you today believe them to be, for people like me, who were schooled in such matters, were observers of the world – not just the natural and the physical elements, but also of human behaviour, that of both individuals and the groups that they formed.

"Thus, slowly, over a long period of time, we developed knowledge, and we recorded this in written form, and through this process, combined with the education of chosen individuals, we passed on our learning from one generation to the next. And in doing this we formed a scholarly community in an otherwise uneducated world. This was the start of learning, which in time evolved into what today you call science, which may in due course itself evolve, once those blinded by the dogma of science open their eyes to how unsophisticated and damaging the modern version of science really is.

"Let me also take this opportunity to put right a misunderstanding about alchemy. You, I expect, think that we spent our time trying to transmute lead into gold and searching for the elixir of eternal life. This is a common misconception. Yes, there were misguided individuals who, believing in the impossible, did seek wealth and immortality. But they were all disappointed, for the quests to transmute lead into gold and for the elixir of eternal life were only figurative; representations of the spiritual dimensions of our ways, whereby we sought, through individual endeavours and a quest for enlightenment, to understand ourselves and our place in the universe, and to live a good life by purifying our thoughts and deeds. Our focus on the spiritual, of bringing this perspective into our observations of life and nature, rested on our belief in the duality of humans; people are more than just animals. This spirituality is the source of the wisdom that we sought to acquire in the quest to develop our understandings of purpose. It is a wisdom that your modern science has lost. And the result is a Godless and soulless world, where you sow the wind and reap the whirlwind, but are too blind to see this.

"Now that I have set the record straight on these matters, I return to Father Christmas. As soon as he halted the sleigh, he told me that I, like him, had been chosen to undertake a special task. He then began to recount his own strange tale, set in the lands north of the Artic Circle, beginning with his setting off into the cold dark forest to collect his yule log, the encounters he experienced on his journey, and ending with his transformation into Father Christmas when he visited the stable in Bethlehem, the occurrence of which I have previously, but only briefly, mentioned in my story. What he wanted most of all to do was to focus my attention on his encounter with the Earth Spirit.

"The Earth Spirit is a phantom that Father Christmas met the night when he left home to collect his yule log. This is a creature that has a philosophy of life totally opposite from that which Father Christmas and I hold to. You will have encountered this creature on your own journey through life, for he has many names; ignorance, want, selfishness, greed, delusion, and dogma, being just a few. His ways are one of existence within a frame of reference devoid of love, caring, giving, sharing, consideration for the needs of others, and so forth. Father Christmas told me of the visions that had been revealed to him by the Earth Spirit. In particular, he wanted me to take note of certain specific matters that concerned my destiny.

"I listened attentively, for he had reached the stage in his intriguing explanation where he revealed to me what I had been selected to do. What he told me was most interesting and, I have to say, deeply disturbing.

"Over the coming centuries, stretching far into the future, further than most people could possibly visualise, three powerful forces would arise in the world, acting towards the improvement and development of humanity. The first of these would be spiritual, the second would be material, and the third would be intellectual. But, he also revealed that each one of these forces was founded on a collection of values and beliefs that would, at times, be subject to corruption and distortion by those who were attracted to these philosophies. In some cases the warping would come from people of evil intent, but in most cases it would be far more insidious, coming instead from those of good intent, but who were blind to the consequences and implications of unthinking application of their values and beliefs. Here he introduced me to a phrase that I have since come across many times: *the road to hell is lined with good intentions.*

"I was then informed that each of these three domains of thought and action would be extremely dangerous and damaging to the development of humankind when so corrupted. And he told me of the huge suffering that would be inflicted on people as a result of the distortions brought about by devotees blinded by dogma.

"Imagine my surprise when, over the centuries, this actually did happen. First it was religion. I do not need to recount here the tale of torture, mutilation, war, and death that has been such a sad part of the many creeds that have developed over the centuries. Then it was the world of business, first through slavery, then through the exploitation of employees, which gave rise to another justification for tyranny and exploitation, this time, perversely, by those who claimed to be acting in the workers' interests. In both cases, spiritual and material, the evil still continues to this day, only its form has changed. Yet again, I do not need to explain here the hatred that stalks the world in the name of religion, and the greed and unethical behaviour of many modern enterprises, both large and small, along with their environmentally damaging actions which many, whether through ignorance or deceit, would have you believe can be dealt with without fundamentally changing purpose and values, and the nature of the economic system.

"What of the third force, the intellectual one? This is just as disappointing as the other two, but in a much more subtle way. First in science, then later in an activity that came to be known as engineering, and in more recent times technology, a very mechanistic and reductionist view of people would take hold, which ultimately would see humans regarded as little more than machines, albeit very complex ones. Worse still, the importance of scientific, engineering and technological facts would begin to dominate, rendering as secondary, or unimportant, human desires, aspirations and feelings. In short, the wishes of ordinary people would no longer be seen as important, or would be treated with contempt by experts, and the world would begin to descend into an existence where only facts produced by experts would be taken into account, and these experts, knowing best, would trample over the aspirations of ordinary people. Perhaps even worse, though, would be the selectivity of facts presented, with only information that supported the various vested interests being taken into account, and the rest, no matter how legitimate, being branded by the label of lack of *right-minded thinking*. The world would become dominated by those who advise in their own interests.

"And such people, some with good intentions, blinded by this narrow view of the world, would eventually and very chillingly express their vision in the form of an infamous statement: *man is a machine, and if he is not, then he is nothing at all.* Thus it would be that those features which make us human would be subsumed to a cold, stark and terrifying world where the lives of people would be determined by experts and technocrats who, knowing best, would decide all matters on the basis of facts and evidence, without regard for what people want.

"You might be wondering, in a tale that is related to Father Christmas, where all this is leading. I will tell you that I also, while sitting in that sleigh, was beginning to wonder the same, for I was by now aware of the task that had been given to this wonderful person. Consequently, having listened politely to what Father Christmas had to say, I was resolved to ask this very question. But I did not need to, for he came to this matter himself in the form of a rhetorical question. 'What,' he asked, 'has this to do with you? Let me explain, for this is what you have been chosen to undertake. This is your destiny.' So I listened with great anticipation.

"Before I reveal to you what he then told me, I want to here remind you that Christmas is ultimately about salvation, not of one individual, but the whole of humankind, and this salvation cannot be attainted if humankind does not break free from the chains that bind people's minds to ideologies, nor if people fail to open their eyes to the dangers inherent in any dogma. Having made this clear, I will say that all rested on the one attribute that I possessed, but which would be absent among those most fervent about their specific dogma, be that religion, economic theory, science, engineering, or technology. What trait, you ask, am I referring to? It is of course wisdom.

"And this is what I was told to do, and what, since that night, I have endeavoured to achieve over the centuries – to bring some wisdom into all these various spheres of human thought. So, taking on many different identities, travelling from one place to another, always careful to move on before anyone became suspicious as to why I did not age, I immersed myself in art, politics, religion, science, engineering, business, often several simultaneously, at all times bringing tolerance, humanity, love and the voice of reason into the world of those inclined towards narrow perspectives, who, I think, find security and certainty in their specific ideology. This, however, is a self-delusion.

"For the most part it has been a frustrating task, speaking to people about that which they have no inclination to listen to or to understand. In most cases people, whether they were priests, scientists, entrepreneurs or engineers, have been unable to comprehend that they are caught up in an ideology which blinds them to the reality of the universe, which is, without doubt, a place of immense diversity and mystery, contrasting sharply with the lack of variety in the minds of the ideologically inclined.

"I must also say, however, that the mission that I have undertaken has not always been an unrewarding one, for there have been a few occasions when I have managed to open people's eyes to larger truths, initiate change in these people's worldviews, and, help them to begin to acquire some wisdom. This gives me hope that all is not yet lost.

"So there you have it, my story, or, to put it another way, the part of the tale of the three wise men that has never been told.

"But, before ending, I want to describe the final matters that Father Christmas revealed to me that night long, long ago. This is the most chilling part of my tale, made more so by my observations that what was revealed to me that night is, I am sure, in these days, coming to pass.

"Father Christmas was, I have to say, no longer jovial and happy when he addressed this subject. He had become serious and concerned as he began to explain that there would come a time when all these three previously mentioned ideological forces would not only increasingly be exerting the damaging side of their influence, but would do so all at the same time and to a degree not previously experienced. More worrying still, they would be bound together in ways that few people would be able to recognise or understand. This, he said, would create very serious problems for humankind, and pose a challenge the like of which would never before have been experienced by the human species; yet most would be blind to this. This, he also informed me, would be an important moment in the human story, and he stressed that I should watch out for this conjunction.

"He went on to explain that I would have no problem recognising when this stage had been reached. I was told that I would begin to think that I was living among lunatics, for the woes of the world would be so obviously connected with these ideological domains, but people would not be stepping back to reflect on the need to change course, but would be advocating more of what was actually causing the challenging circumstances to which he was alluding. He also told me that the world by this time would have developed into what would seem to be a very sophisticated place, but that this would in fact just be an illusion, for human thought would still be trapped in the past.

"His final words were that my hitherto unrestricted freedom to move about and go where I pleased to restart my life, would come to an end, for the world would become dominated by what he called the Nation State, although at that time I did not know what he meant by this term. I was informed that the leaders of these countries would become obsessed with security, fearing not just other countries, but also evil individuals and groups who would be the blind children of ideology, and whose distortions and corruptions of basically good philosophies would be self-evident. Leaders of nations would, he said, also be considerably worried by their inability to confirm the identity of their citizens, and would resort to monitoring, tracking and controlling everyone, while insisting on knowing details about individuals that no sane person would want their leaders and governments to know. Yet few would object.

"I asked him what would be the outcome for humanity when this dangerous period in human development was reached. He said he did not know, and what is more, he did not want to know, which left me feeling very ill at ease. And

I have to say that these final words have haunted me ever since.

"You can imagine that I have had plenty of time to reflect on this matter and I have also encountered, over the centuries, many people who have foolishly predicted the end of the world, yet life goes on. I am wise, hence I know not to make such predictions, but in many respects it would be better for you all if such end-of-the-world prophecies were to one day come true, for death will seem a better alternative to the hell that ideology will have created.

"I conclude by stating that I am certain that humanity, metaphorically speaking, is approaching the *gates of hell*, and very soon, if not already, you will find yourselves on the threshold of the point of no return. But, lest I end on too pessimistic a note, I will present a few words of hope by quoting from another well known Christmas story: *'men's courses will foreshadow certain ends, to which, if preserved in, they must lead, but if the courses be departed from the ends will change.'*

"As I have already mentioned, Christmas is ultimately about salvation, and this comes in many different forms. It is time for humankind to begin to grow up and to once again actively seek wisdom, while the option to change course is still open."

The End